SINGING MY OWN SONG

SINGING MY OWN SONG

SYIEVE LOCKLAIR

Singing My Own Song: Poetry in the Key of Love

First Printing, 2025

ISBN: 979-8-218-71591-5
Ebook ISBN: 979-8-218-71593-9

589 Print Publications

For and In Memory of
Whitney Houston

...

*The Voice.
The Heavenly songbird that serenaded our souls
before soaring to a higher Home;
you are truly an angel.
Thank you for the music, the memories,
and the milestones.
The history. The inspiration.
Gone far too soon, but never shall you be forgotten.
My love is your love.*

To those who've:

hurt me, loved me, tried to hold me down,
supported me, walked away from me, stood by me,
and to those who stride by me
and those who always ride with me.
Without you, I wouldn't be me.

Contents

The Secret — 1

Through The Times — 2

Reality Check — 4

Semblance — 5

Quitclaim Heart — 7

Sing My Song — 9

Relax. Relate. Release. — 12

Progress — 14

Into Thin Air — 16

[blank stare] — 19

No Shame In My Game — 22

When I Said Goodbye — 24

The One and Only — 27

I Don't Hurt Anymore — 29

Behind Me — 31

In A Word — 34

BrokeHeart Hill — 36

Fog + Mist — 38

The Discontentment of Severance — 39

A-Game — 42

I Say Goodbye to You   43

You've Been Warned   45

Go In and Let Have   46

Love Alarmed   48

Passing The Torch   50

Damn You   52

Throwing In The Towel   54

With Open Eyes   56

Self   58

On A Mission   60

Christmas Without You: The Special Times   62

Christmas Without You: Underneath The Tree   65

Christmas Without You: One Wish   67

Christmas Without You: The Present Is The Gift   69

Inishedfay   71

Ma Winda Pain   74

The Work   76

Mirror, Mirror   78

Iron In The Fire   81

Auric   83

Pink Posty   84

I Got Me   85

Glow   86

"Goodbye" [in French]   87

POW!!!   88

Pushing Up Daisies   89

180   91

Shoo   93

Oil + Vinegar	95
Antiquity	98
I.HATE.YOU.	100
You Don't Even Know	102
Get	104
Closure Letter	106
Objects	108
Love Into Being	109
Fed Up	111
One of Those Moments	113
Victory	114
Two Cents' Worth	115
Forever Came	116
#Swerve	118
raison d'être	120
ROI (Return On Investment)	123
No Longer	125
Miss Me, I'm Gone	126
It's Over	127
Over My Shoulder	128
You In Us	130
Me Because of You	132
You	134
"I Love You, Back!"	136

1

The Secret

This
You could never be
When your schedule's consumed with jealousy
Of me
To achieve
You have to be fabulous and free
Which isn't made for just anybody
To me, it's easy
Comes naturally
Let me tell you a little something
Help you ease your mind
I am one of a kind
I am reason; I am rhyme
Collectively and individually
Me...You could never be

2

Through The Times

There are things in my heart
Things I want you to know
Things that are tearing me apart
Things like how it feels to love someone on a level
And not be able to let it show
For it's a level they can't handle
And the same level that leaves you hurt and disheveled

There are times you leave me speechless
And thoughts of you leave me sleepless
There are times when I want to surrender, for you defeat me
Times when feelings for you consume and deplete me
Leaving me feeling like I can't go on; like I don't belong
Exhausted to the point where I sing someone else's song
For they seem to tell my story for the present times
Those times...those moments...that used to be mine
The instances where I could easily express myself through rhyme

If one day I should lose my mind
Taking myself beyond wit's end

You know how
You are why
The day we met...that's the when
And yet, the day after, I'll still be loving you
Loving you for a long time
Cause, it seems I have loved you for the longest time
But, it's one time only; never again
When it ends; it will be...the end

3

Reality Check

To feel my heart stop
To feel my soul shake
To feel my spirit set itself on fire
To feel the agony as I engulf in flames
To feel my hope evaporate and my dream shatter
To feel the moment I realized that to you I didn't matter
The instant life with the one I love fell dead
Chest heavy; head bowed in dread
Staring at a puddle of blood that's bled
An injury from the words you said
The pain of which I couldn't take
Yet, it helped me accept loving you as a mistake

Now, I dim my spot, as the light's no longer lime
And fly away from you; testifying, I will do better next time

4

Semblance

I'm the one you let go
Willingly. Thoughtlessly.
I slipped through your fingers
I fell through the cracks

Now, you're training others to walk in my tracks
Looking at rings, talking about things
Discussing my kind of plans
Your madness doesn't faze me
Just so you know
I'm actually enjoying this masquerade of a show

Don't push me aside like I'm a watered-down drink
Don't treat me like I'm a second place prize
When I'm the first thought you think
Each morning you rise
The reason for the tears in each of your eyes

You see my face
When you notice someone walking down the street

When you close your eyes at night to get some sleep
What can I say?
Try as you may
You'll never find another to take my place
Years down the road and many lovers later
We both know, you won't have anyone better
Just a knock-off, a wanna-be, a slightly irregular

5

Quitclaim Heart

Don't pretend to be my friend
Period; full stop. This chapter's at its end
Tomorrow's a new day; new books we'll begin
Exhale, inhale; let us breathe again

The gate is open; the path is clear
There's no need for me to have you here
I'd rather you be gone
Than to have you here and I still be alone
Take in life's landscape...be free; explore
No longer trapped in a friendship you don't want anymore

I see the pain in your eyes when you look at me
I feel the sadness that surrounds us in moments you used to touch me
In times we're together...you're unhappy
This isn't working for me; too unhealthy

I am learning to live without the love you weren't able to give
I'm taking a step and making a change

Setting us free
Asking you to do the same
Do it for me and do it for yourself
While I want you here, you'll be better somewhere else

Our final act; never one of selfishness:
Shake hands...and walk away from this

6

Sing My Song

Lovers, like friends
They come and they go
I remember the moment I met you
I know the moment I lost you
Now is the moment I have to stop loving you

Baby, I know I deserve a greater man
But there are things about being in love I've yet to understand
Crazy how I'll get down on my knees and beg you, please
Baby, please don't leave
When it's the one thing I need you to do
For the day to come when I open my eyes and realize
You're not that golden prize
Curse me for the halo I placed upon your head
Sacrificed my happiness for a love you wouldn't give
Lost my soul just to see you smile
And to be in your presence, if only for a little while

Honey, why can't I let go
When you want to be somewhere else

Why can't I let go
When I need to free myself
Baby why
Why can't I just let go
When your love
Will never grow
Why can't I let you go
When your love
It will never show
And it's Your Love I'll never know

I walk towards you; you pull away
I aim to kiss you; your eyes turn gray
And your lips say it's not okay
Your stare looks straight through me
Your hands never touch my body
I try to protect you from the winter cold
But your feelings for me, boy I've never been told
You're next to me; you're everywhere I turn
You'll give me nothing; I've come to learn

Your warmth is chilling; unnervingly
Empty-handedness doesn't work for me
I've told you so
Neither a rock I can run to
Nor a shoulder I can lean on
If you won't be my angel; you won't be my hero

Someone tell me why
Why I'd rather die than let you go
I want you; I need you near
Don't break my heart
Simply do your best; play your part

Talk to me
Tease me
Whisper
Sweetly
Gently...in my ear
Tell me baby
Tell me that you love me
Or tell me, baby...why you here?

7

Relax. Relate. Release.

Our eyes locked; our fingers intertwined
Stop it; you know you're mine
Free your inhibitions
Embrace your intentions
Our bodies yearn
Our emotions burn
Place your hands upon me
Caress my body
Ignite my fire
Satisfy my soul
Do the things I like that nobody knows
Taste me from my earlobes down to and between my toes
Explore every nip
Every crevice
Every dip
Make me quiver
Feel me shiver
Whisper those nasty, filthy, dirty words
Make me blush before they're said
Take me to the mountaintop

The moment I beg you not to stop
That instance of ecstasy when my eyes roll back into my head
Give it to me
Give me all you got
Turn me out
Make me shout
Push me over that highest peak
Make my tongue rattle and roll when I try to speak
Kiss me
Taste me
Become one with me
Press into me
Open your heart
Have no fear
Smile from ear to ear
Release a joyous, single tear
Hold me
Take me
Let's give each other what we need
Come, baby
Give me your .....

8

Progress

The marathons I've run
The mountains I've moved
The oceans I've swam
The walls I've climbed
The obstacles I've overcome
And the bridges I've burned
My life
An endless journey of learning, accomplishment, and pain
A better me for all that I've lost and for all that I have gained
I love me for all that I am

I ran, I hid
I protected myself from me
I covered and I camouflaged the me that nobody knew
Traveled life's path, searching for the history of me
Found love for myself and happiness within
Now, I'm sharing my story
Telling it from the beginning; before it ends
The way it's supposed to be
I'm singing my own song

And writing the music to go along
Redefining Me; becoming my own man
I'm loving me for who I am

A real love, a true love
Flowing abundantly and freely
Lifting me higher
Taking me over and above the trivial
The meaningless, the minor
Dedicated devotion, endless support, and friendship
I know and I love me
Wide open
No shame
Standing on my mountaintop, shouting my own name
Smiling. Dancing.
Like no one's and everyone's watching
Endless seconds of fame
I'm still me
Better, lovely...all the same.

I love me like no one else can
I, now, know...who and all I Am

9

Into Thin Air

Said you never meant to hurt me
Claimed you didn't mean for me to cry
Spoke a lot of nothing
And I still don't know the reason why
Why me? Why us?

I've come to realize your love was in vain
I know you won't apologize or alleviate the pain
So, I'll spare my breath and won't put up a fuss
But how could you walk away?
How could you just disappear?
No kiss
No hug
No thought
No happy goodbye

What do you expect better than me to be?
I gave you my all
All you'd ever need
More than you could ever want

I quenched your thirst
I satisfied your hunger
I supplied your appetizer
I became your dessert
I was your three-course meal
I gave you the best, baby
A lot better than the rest
It saddens me to know you'll settle for less
Careless whispers
Thoughtless kisses
Depreciated; valueless
A second-rate companionship; economy class
Why have reflux when you can have deluxe
That's just regurgitated madness
But, I digress
The love I gave you, wasn't a fraction of my best
You're the reason I proclaim: no baggage on my plane
Get off the highway; you're too slow for the fast lane
And no good for the right lane

I sang your praises on high
I took you seriously
You took me for granted
Didn't take us at all
Just turned around
Without a trace or a sound
No kiss
No wave
No sigh
No expressed goodbye

No claim to reign supreme
But I am le crème de la crème

Highest quality; the finest cream
When you open your eyes
You'll know...I was your dream

This is the road you chose
Travel it
The bed you made
Sleep in it
The hole you dug
Wallow in it
See me from afar
Think of what could have been
If you hadn't turned and walked into air so thin
No kiss
No respect
No decency
No simple goodbye

I hope you choke.

10

[blank stare]

From the roots of the American south
To the distant lands of Japan
I've been a lot of places
Gone from city to town
Seen lots of faces
And, yet, here I am

I stand here
Looking at you
To show me you care
Waiting for you
To say you want me here
Here I stand
With a stare upon my face
Wanting you to invite me into your space
Hoping for you to touch me there
Desiring for us to be near
Longing to know your embrace

Here I am; standing, staring blankly

When I should be tossing you a side-eye glance
My inner voice screams then yells
Trying to free me from my trance
"What the hell?"
"This is no romance!"
"Break the spell!"
"Ratchetness at its highest!"
"Satchet."
"Turn away…"
"Let the broken-heart pieces lay as they fell."

Your touch is like steel and iron
Cold. Hard. Rusted.
Deprivation at its best.
My love is like diamonds and titanium
Exquisite. Clear. Raw.
A premium.

Blankly, I stand
In your world
I don't exist
Yet, you, I can't resist
I'm last on your list
Uninvited on your guest list
Your mother's never heard my name
Your coworkers know nothing about me
To your friends, I'm just a piece in your game
You're all in my world
My pretzel's twist
Sadly unparalleled; we don't view us the same

I stare as I stand
I'm tired. Exhausted.

My last leg is run.
My soul feels empty
My emotions are depleted
Without fighting you I'm defeated

I'll still be here
Standing for you
I'll be the rock you run to
The shoulder you cry on
The friend on which you depend

Standing...staring...
Gaining my second wind.

No Shame In My Game

I don't hate you
But, I don't love you like I used to
Apparently, you feel the same
It's been two years
You haven't called one time
Yet, I still sit by the phone
Waiting on it to ring
Each time, wanting it to be you on the line
Unsure if you think I'm worth the dime

It's hard to fathom, but it's clear
I'm the one for whom you're too busy to find time
Better known as "the last one on your mind"
The one you can turn your back on
Walk out on
Stop loving
Without reason or rhyme
And live guilt-free as if it's not a crime

There are still things left to be said

Conversations I long for
Discussions you dread
Steps to take for our differences to be resolved
Decisions on how our relationship should evolve

You're doing you
And I'm doing me
Yet, there are times when I find myself thinking of us
And how we used to be
Things aren't the same
People
Life
Love
Relationships
They change.

If you need me
Reach out to me
Dial my number
Say my name
Just think of me
I'll come running
Hail, shine, snow, or rain
Avalanche
Tornado
Earthquake
Hurricane

12

When I Said Goodbye

There comes a time when you realize a dream will never be
Like me being in love with you and you in love with me
A reality deferred
It just wasn't meant to be
Loving me, for you, was never true

I said goodbye to give you space and preserve face
To let wounds heal
To let seeds grow
To shield my heart from someone who didn't want it
But couldn't find the words to say so

I couldn't continue wasting my energy
On a love that wasn't going to be
Looking into my eyes didn't change your mind
It didn't even brighten up your day
The sight of my tears stirred no emotion in your face
With every word, every sound, and every moment you didn't
touch me
My hope faded away

The time came for you to talk to me from behind
To look at my footprints
As I no longer stood, but moved on
Getting myself to solid ground
You gave no reason to stay
You didn't even try to keep me from walking away
Goodbye was all that was left to say that day

It was tough
Knowing that for you I wasn't enough
Living each day being something you didn't want
I couldn't do anything to change the way you felt
That was pain; that was real
It turned my soul into steel
But my heart was like flesh inflicted with a welt

When I said goodbye
The time had come for me to heal
I had played the fool for far too long
What I'd wish was right was so wrong

When I said goodbye
It was my way of saying what you couldn't express
Like a lost love letter
Without a return address

When I said goodbye
It was time for me to right this wrong
No more wanting you to play along
No more wishing to you I belonged
No more singing my tired song

When I said goodbye
It was another perfect gift
From me to you
Then, I had no clue
But, now, it makes sense in hindsight view

When I said goodbye
I knew I would be bolting the door
I knew there would be pain in store
When I said goodbye
I knew...it would hurt me more

13

The One and Only

Don't promise me the stars
Don't bring me the sun
I don't need diamonds; just roses and real words
To feel you beyond the dreams
Seduce me; make me see heaven in your eyes

I want to touch and feel you
Kiss you, taste you
Make love to you with my eyes
To be next to you
To get to know you
To be a part of you

I want to feel your hands on my body
My lips kissing yours
Your scent relaxing me
Our emotions entwined
Our bodies entangled
Sensually
I ache for you

I want to be your one and only
The end to each other's life journey
Destiny fulfilled
Complete bliss

Reality has set in
I think of you all the time
I'm sure I don't cross your mind
I've never met your family or your friends
Yet, you know all of mine

I want my smile to run through you
To warm you from within

I'm all around you, but you don't see me
Can I be overlooked that easily?

The things I say don't touch you
The actions I take don't move you
I can't see our sun through your rain
I can't feel the joy for the pain
I try to love and hold you tight
You run away; all kinds of wrong
Get your life right
Realize we belong

I want to be the one who...
The only who...
Your One.
Your Only.

14

I Don't Hurt Anymore

My heart broke when I lost you
The loudest sound I've ever heard
I didn't know what I would do
I couldn't find me for losing you

No more lost sleep
I feel wonderful, now
Too many nights I cried
A few times I wanted to die
Knowing I cared for you
And you not feeling the same in return
The suffering and the pain I went through
My lesson has been learned

Your love was a drug
A burdensome storm
I went through it to get through it

Your weight has been lifted
I survived it all

Thankful I never crumbled
I came out on top somehow

I don't hurt anymore
I feel good now
My light inside shines brightly
There's a burning love deep inside me
Putting me on top
No one will ever come before it
No one will ever make it stop
It fills me up and keeps giving me more
I feel good, baby
I don't hurt anymore

I thought I had lost me along the way
But, I'm doing well and I feel good
Living my life like it's golden
The way I should
Smiling from ear to ear

Eyes bright
Skin glowing
My sexy is tight
My vibe is right
It's like the stars are shining just for me
And the earth spins just to keep me near
Pain? I'm not doing that anymore
I feel good; like never before

15

Behind Me

You'd been dead to me for so long
I'd written new lyrics, found a new band, and started singing
a new hit song
One that makes you feel good and makes you wanna dance along

Then like a change in beat
A songstress crooning in the wrong key
I feel your presence
Around me
Surrounding me
Powering into me
I turned around...
And my world stopped

My face a solid frown
Looking into your eyes
Glowing, gleaming
Nothing but a smile
Staring; silently
Waiting for me to say the first word

To break the silence
To say the words from you I never heard

Trapped.
Knowing I should bow out; gracefully, somehow

Intrigued.
Deep inside my soul sports a smile
Yet, I know this time I spend with you will be worthless in a while

It felt like yesterday when I couldn't love me right for trying to
love you more
I lost sight of what was in sight
Right in front of me
Rooted, deeply within me
Too much time wasted on you
Too much energy spent trying to be with you
When you wouldn't let me love you
When you didn't want me to

You left, but my love stayed
It wore me out; made me doubt
Hurt my heart
Made me cry
Made me shout
Took me through agony and back again
Trying to understand what you were all about
I wanted to rise higher, not fall into the fire
Engulfed in my own flames

So, to stand here
Looking at you
Wanting to hate you

Wanting to hug you
Wanting to know who's to blame
There's anger
There's hurt
There's sadness
There's shame
Then suddenly realizing
You're in front of me
Yet, you're behind me
Nothing's the same

My love has died
That place you occupied is now empty
I like you, but I don't love you
I've done well without you

We can be friendly
Or we can be friends

Maybe.

16

❧

In A Word

I said "Yes"
"Yes" ... and "Yes"
"Ohhhhh YES!"

I have to...
It's time to go
I can no longer be here for you
Trying to solve your problems
When I have my own
One of which is you
The rest relate to you

To myself, I have to be true

For years you've been giving me the nice words
But, I've yet to hear the right words
I thought I was here to stay
But I can't go on this way

I love the things you do

But you've yet to touch me with what you say

No one else can do what you do to me
I can't take you doing it anymore, either, baby
I gotta go
I gotta rescue me

Because of you, I'm standing in my own way
I have to love myself
I have to create my destiny
I have to pull myself together and walk away

So deep in your tunnel of love
I couldn't see my way out to the other side
After all the years I cried
I had to open my eyes and realize
I don't need to be where I'm not wanted
A pain I've finally confronted

I release myself from your hold
I am strong, I am bold
Never thought I'd see this day
The moment I say "NO"
You are free; you can go
I am no longer a thorn in your side
I open the door
I open it wide
No us
No more

17

BrokeHeart Hill

Tears in my eyes
Emptiness in my soul
Cold in my spirit
Anger in my mind
Hollowness in my voice

Atop a hill of heartache and pain
Sometimes I just want to jump
Find a way to end it all
I wish I could unlove you
I wish I'd never loved you at all
You touched my heart in so many places
I see your smile on so many faces

It doesn't matter what I do
It doesn't matter where I turn
You're embedded in my soul
To be with you; I constantly yearn
My anger, my desire – they burn

It's not leaving
I'm not going
Wrapped up in love like I'll never have it, again
Wanting nothing more than to wear your name
About to lose myself agonizing over why you don't feel the same

My life's upside down; everything's changed
Each day I spend trying to let you go
You were the first
You should have been my last
You were the one I wanted to spend my life with
The garden, the garage
The white picket fence
The weekend getaways
The nights of love and suspense
The mornings of delight and satisfaction
I could have been bored out of my mind
But moments with you were like floating on Cloud Nine

I sit here staring into the setting sun
Trying to think of the right things to say
The right things to do
To do whatever it takes

My mind is undone...
Thoughts of you
Feelings for you
Memories with you
They won't go away

Destroyed by a love unreturned
You may have won the battle
But you won't get the best of me

18

Fog + Mist

It's getting, not having, that pleases you

To think of you. To look at you. To be near you.
Ignites an internal combustion
A fiery discombobulation fueled by exhaustion
Surrounding the confusion of our union
The mixed emotions regarding us
Provided by you. Sponsored by you. Courtesy of you.

You say you want me
But you don't
You want to walk away from me
But you won't

Desire keeps you here
Rage. Anxiety. Intrigue.
Keep you near

19

The Discontentment of Severance

I waited for you for far too long
Wanting to hear you sing my song
Then life painted a picture
A picture where I didn't belong
A scene where the space between us was far and strong
It helped me find my point to pack up and move along

Yet, my spirit isn't free
It's holding on to you
Recalling how we were once two
Blocking a miracle that's meant for me
The blessing of not being attached to you

I try to let you go
While my heart keeps hanging on
I'm past wanting to love you
Yet your presence seems to linger

I try to move beyond
But envision your ring upon my finger

Your kisses have long been gone
I'm a distant memory to you
Not a thought that comes your way
I'm filled with so much anger
Overflowing with so much pain
My heart beats for nothing
All my feelings are in vain
I'm holding on to memories
And making wishes I can't explain

Your words are promises from you
But your actions don't come through
Disappointment materializes
I realize I should let go
But I have faith in you
I still believe

You gave me that great beginning
It's like I'm holding out for my fairy-tale ending
The ever-after
'Til death do us part

I know that I can't have you
I know that I don't love you
But, I can't...
I don't know how...

I don't know how to let you go.

But, I will

I will learn it
I will claim it
I will live it

Tomorrow, you will be someone I used to know

20

A-Game

Don't practice on me
Know your strategy
Come complete
Come to compete
I'm the championship, baby
Be the MVP
I only roll VIP

21

I Say Goodbye to You

I'm not running after you to tell you I love you
When you run away and stay away from me
Won't talk to me, won't call me
No texts received from you to me
You do nothing but ignore me when I reach out to you
If you wanted me, you'd meet me halfway
Something simple; like normal people do

I'm not chasing after you to tell you I miss you
I'm done spending energy running after you
Just to be friendly to you
When you treat me like trash
It's not even worth being friends with you
I'm done
I won't be a fool
I'll let you be an ass

I'm not waiting for you to come around
You left me, you don't need me
Nothing's gonna change

My pride remains
My dignity's intact
Even if you wanted to
You can't come back
I wrote and I co-sign that

No more doing what I used to do
From here, I say goodbye to you
You go on; you do you
I got me, myself; and, I don't need you

22

You've Been Warned

My love is priceless and my emotions will stop you in your tracks
My revenge is incomparable
My forgiveness; unattainable
My forgetting...unimaginable

Don't fuck up.

23

Go In and Let Have

Don't make me go in and let have
I'll show you how it's done
Play if you want to
But, I am not the one

I will bless your soul so badly
You'll think we're in church
Lost between testifying, praying, and passing the Collection Plate
Jumpin', shoutin', hootin', hollerin'
Praising...dancing from foot to foot

Magnolia beautiful
Solid as a southern oak
My branches span oceans wide
Unprecedented shade
I deliver

Go on and get yours
If I come in, you're getting mine
I keep you in check

Yes, I'm that kind
School of Spare the Rod
and You'll Lose Your Mind

No doubts about it
I give you what you ask
Trim the fat, toss the skinny
Put me first; I'll be your last
When I dish, I serve
Top...Down

When all is said and I am done
You're like water under a bridge
A bridge that's been burned and ashes blown away
Salty
Still

I go in.
I let have.
I slay.

24

Love Alarmed

In order to endure it
I had to go through it
I was strong enough to love you
I'm stronger for living without you

It was a long and burning journey
Now; I cry, but it's not because of pain
I've known love before
I'll know it once again

Where truths go unspoken
Lay things we'll never know

You were better for me
But, I am no longer selfish
Spread your wings; fly away from this
Go be your best with someone else

Your love is the closest I've ever known
How foolish of me to want it all on my own

I've imagined myself wearing your ring
Wrapped in love; hyphenating your name
But; when it rains, it pours
Windows shattered; busted doors
Rooms filled with smoke
Walls blazing; everything's on fire
Thick tension that could choke
Those final seconds; down to the wire
I was about to lose my breath
And cook my own goose
When all hell broke loose

But, I survived
I put out the blaze
Bruised, but not broken
I'm alive
From here on, I will thrive

25

Passing The Torch

I could never see clearly
For what I wanted to actually be
Everything in place; perfect harmony
Me with him and him with me

Then came you; strolling along
Stealing the spotlight
Singing the right song

Sharp and focused
Is my past when it's in hindsight view
Hitting me upside my head
Smacking me in my face
Absorbing the obvious that was somehow missed
Bringing the truth down upon me, putting me in the right space

The signs were everywhere
The things that were said
The things that were done
None said "I care"

None said "You're the One"
Gave no reason for me to be there
A game that couldn't be lost or won

He walked away from me; back into his past
I stood there expecting his return
Endless waiting to give my all, my best, my last
Each day fueling my love's burn
It would be too late by the time I did learn

Months go by...and not one word
I'm perched here; and he's nowhere around
A blip on the radar; a motion on the screen
He's changed directions
For me, what does that mean?

He's doing something new
Let's call that something You
Holding on to what looks to be true
My heart and my soul turning all shades of blue

I'll take the high road
And do something classy
I'll release the hold I have on him
And give My Love to you

Treat him well
Do right by him
You're where I should have been

Cupcake wishes.
Cashmere kisses.

26

Damn You

There was a time when I thought it might've been me
But who are we kidding
It's you
And all the stupid shit you do
Send a text when you should call
When you could text...
Yep...silence.
Don't hear from your sorry ass at all
Take a note: we all find time for things we want to do
So, "I was busy" as your excuse for your lack of follow-through
Take that elsewhere and come at me with something new
Forget borrowed
And don't even think about blue
Try true

Stop accusing me of lecturing
And riding your back
Get yourself in check
And don't give me reasons to attack
It's plain and it's simple

Come correct

Don't bring me foolishness
And keep the drama
I am sick of the somethings
If it's not one thing; it's another
I could love you incessantly
But I won't baby you like I'm your mama
Open your mouth.
Communicate.
Speak your line
I can be psychotic, but I have never been psychic
I don't read minds
And I'm not sifting through your bullshit
To extract reason from rhyme
Or separate fiction from fact
I hereby solemnly swear...
It's official
It's a pact
Don't come at me with that

The craziness; it's like a circle
It never ends
From the past to the present
And back, again
All kinds of asses
All kinds of "them"
Same old tired lines
Just different days and different times
Get your life
I got mine

27

Throwing In The Towel

When I walk away from you, will you shed a tear?
How long will it take before you have someone else here?
A second?
A minute?
An hour?
A day?
Rehearsing my lines
Imitating my moves
Trying to fill my custom-made shoes

I look into your eyes and I see my face
A moment of clarity and understanding
Anyone could be standing in my place
How did we get here?
Tell me when
Tell me how
You used to love me, but you can't stand me, now

Nothing hurts like knowing I mean nothing to you when you once
thought I was someone special

Or is that not true?
Have I been just another one to you?
A pastime?
A distraction?
Someone for you to kick it with and spend some occasional time?
A sideline.

After all I've been through
All the things I thought I knew
Now, suddenly, I don't think I do
I rewrite the story but it always ends the same
It's boring me
It's destroying me
This pattern can't remain

I've done it all and given you my best
I'm laying my burdens down and putting us to rest
No more holding on
I'm letting go so I can keep growing
Moving on
Being better
Staying strong
Doing what I need to do
No longer living and breathing you
You'll be better without me
And I'll be my best without y.o.u.

28

With Open Eyes

I imagined you loving me completely
Accepting my flaws and all
Catching me when I would fall
Carrying me when I could only crawl
Purifying my air, giving me breath to breathe
Taking my hand and holding my heart
Being my lover, my supporter, and my friend
From early-morning's sunrise to late-night's end
But that was back when....

I never thought I'd say this, but I'm better off without you
You only aimed to fulfill my material fantasies
You were there, but not for me
You were never connected with me or concerned about me
What you gave, I provided for myself
I didn't need that from anyone else

I gave you all of me
I fulfilled your needs
I became your fantasy

I satisfied you exhaustively
I gave you strength when you were weak
Yet, you didn't appreciate me
You pushed me away with the things you needed to say but
would not speak

I prayed and asked for hands to be laid upon me
To guide me in the direction back to you
Or to give me the strength to leave you alone
I was catching hell being with you, but still being on my own

You never know what you have until it's gone
Maybe not now, but someday...somehow
You'll realize how much you miss me
How much you need me
How much you loved me
How much value you had in me
How you will never do better than me

29

Self

People often ask me how I do it
It's simple...I'm me
I live life like it's shiny and golden
As if glitter flickers just for me
I turn pieces into peace
I am not perfect
But I am not broken

I love me
I cherish me
I put me first
I am honest, I am open
I am direct
I trim the excess and serve the necessary
I communicate
I don't tolerate chaos and I don't do stress
I have yet to determine the benefits of wallowing in
someone else's mess

There are lessons in difficult situations

Wisdom to be learned
Courage to be earned
What about it reflects me?
What can I take away from this?
There's always a silver lining
What's dark and gray to others
Is metallic to me

I don't let trouble weigh me down
I don't let it make me frown
It's become a source that makes me stronger
I used to be afraid I would tumble
But, I am a prisoner of challenge no longer
There are times when I stumble
But I pick myself up
 I vow not to crumble

There's this thing deep inside
It provides you with essentials
All that you could need
Find it
Hold it
Cherish it
Feed it
With it, you will survive

I call it Love
Not love for a lover
Not love for a family member or a friend
But love for yourself...unconditionally, without end

Be you. Do you.
Embrace you. Love you.

30

On A Mission

That hunger; craving unceasingly
Scouting for that perfect delight
A quest, a journey
Like a predator on its prey; about to strike
Our eyes engaged the second they met
The plan was sealed, locked, and set

No mystery; what would be would be
Not too crass, not too flirty
Not too nice, not too dirty
You figured out what I wanted and gave it to me

Half hour
Midnight
The entire night gone

Moments of endless ecstasy
Moments of you
Moments of me
Moments of fun anew

Moments yesterday we never thought would be

The lights were off, but we were on
Teddy.
Marvin.
Luther.
Melodies for every moan

Ignited from the places you gently kissed
My ankles, my hips, my crevices, my lips
Never too much focus on any one place
Making my head spin and my body rejoice
No regrets; this was a choice
Satisfied, not bowed in disgrace
Head up, shoulders back, giving good face

Naomi, eat your heart out
You have nothing on this
A player in the Grown & Sexy Game
Catwalking; not the Walk of Shame

The deed is done
No need to lay blame
On me, on you, or anyone
We played
We conquered
We came

31

Christmas Without You: The Special Times

I'm wishing the phone to ring or a text to appear
Revealing your thoughts of me this time of year
Wishing me happiness and holiday cheer

Outside, the snow is falling
The streetlights are glowing
Our stockings have been hung
And the candles are lit
I'm on the floor by the fire like we used to sit
Reflecting over the years
Reminding myself of the moments when you were here
We'd be wrapped in each other
Our arms holding us tight
Smiling
Laughing
Kissing
All through the night
While soulful carols filled our ears

Giving us comfort and warmth that made Perfect feel just right

Now, you're there and I'm here
Staring into an empty flame
Wishing things were still the same
Silent nights are strange and new
I shouldn't be Christmasing if I have to do it without you

You chose another
Over the treasure I gave
A gift that wasn't bought
Just true and from the heart
In-exchangeable
Non-transferable
Intangible
A part of me to you
Your gift to me, I can't take
Pain shouldn't be delivered via heartbreak
Our bond – like broken glass – shattered
Instantaneous to you, it's like we never mattered
It's hurtful to know you're happy and smiling
You've completely moved on
While I'm still rejecting the fact that you're gone

These few weeks in November and December
These were our special times
The one's we'd cherish and remember
Where we reflected on the past – the sunsets and storms
we weathered
And discussed the future – dreamed of all we'd do together
Creating magic that would last along the way
Now, it's me sitting here
Struggling to accept that I'm by myself

And you're making love and memories with someone else

How can this time mean nothing to you
Lit the candles with you standing behind me
We strung garland around the tree
Kissed each Christmas morning underneath the mistletoe
That we would hang in the doorway Thanksgiving Day

You walked away without a trace
Your footsteps have been blanketed by snow
Just a trail running down my face
Eyes full of tears
Heart full of sorrow
Spirit devoid of emotion
My mouth filled with words I don't have the strength to say
Deeply shocked; not knowing what to do
I don't know Christmas, when it comes without you

32

Christmas Without You: Underneath The Tree

Your presents are under the tree
Wrapped with love
Wrapped with care
Just sitting there

I want to mail them
I want to burn them
I want you to have them
Not that you would care

My presents and presence used to put a smile on your face
Your laugh would ignite me deep inside
I'd melt uncontrollably from your strong embrace
Looking into your eyes, I could see the oceans and the
stars – a heaven for me to float in

I long to be where you are; standing by your side
Living the holiday spirit

Celebrating the old
Welcoming the new
I'd give anything to be next to you
Christmas isn't Christmas
Doing it without you

33

Christmas Without You: One Wish

I wish that you were here
To wipe my tears
And to silence my cries
Whatever I did to make you leave
I apologize
I don't need presents or gifts
Leisures or luxuries
Just you
Here holding me
Laughing with me
Hugging me
Dancing with me
Loving me while I love you

We had each other...
We were each other...
Each other's strength
Each other's voice

Each other's hope
Each other's drive
Each other's mountain to lean on
Each other's shoulder to cry on
Each other's paradise
Me for you
You for me
Just me and you; the two
Kissing and cuddling each night through

My only wish this year
Is for you to be here
Me holding you near

It's Christmas Eve
For tomorrow's sunrise
You should awaken to look into my eyes
But, you're with someone who isn't me
If I'm not happy, you shouldn't be
I'm lonely and blue
Holidays aren't special
When the celebration is without you

34

Christmas Without You: The Present Is The Gift

Mere days until the New Year
There's something about the day
Of new and fresher beginnings
That make it all seem so clear
The sense of purpose
The sense of self
The sense of freedom
The ability to be free
A rebirth into a new me
A state that's feared by many

Maintain control in all you do
Never give anyone reign over you
Realize lovers come and lovers will go
The when's, the where's
The why's, the how's
Reasons we never know

Pain rises more than it subsides
Raindrops will fall
Flowers will grow
Leaning on someone prohibits you from standing tall
Loving yourself is the greatest gift of all

35

Inishedfay

I'm not drunk
I'm brokenhearted and blurry eyed
I'm pissed
It's difficult, it's shameful, it's sad
Remembering trying to walk down this very street
In those moments following the time when bliss met defeat
Mumbling thoughts I failed to speak
Emotions my mouth wouldn't evacuate
Trying to block words that entered through my ears
Barricading the oceans that threatened tears

Now, I'm looking at you
And you're looking at me
We're looking at our watches
Guessing who'll be the first to speak
Your eyes are smiling; I'm always the one with something to say
But I've waited a while for this, I can give you another day

You're uncomfortable being around me
Your discomfort makes me sweat

Words have been thrown
Bridges have been burned
I still don't know how here did we get
It's scary how being with you is still so easy

You were once my everything
I wanted to be your all
Just being around you made my heart sing
Then something happened
We failed to rise before the fall

You broke the news after you poured the coffee
French Roast to be exact
You dug right in and said what needed to be said
No consideration; minor compassion and tact
I looked around for the sugar and the cream
My hands shook
And there was no butter for my bread
This couldn't be happening, I thought it was a dream

You wanted something light; not too heavy, not too dark
You know...fun
Something with someone other than me
A connection with someone; chemistry
First with someone before me
Then with someone after me
Turns out...with anyone...but me

I've finally gotten what I wanted
The reason that I was never told
The truth from you to me
The words that would set me free
Release the hold

I'm over it

This issue is closed.

36

❦

Ma Winda Pain

Stop lookin' through ma winda
Actin' like ya wanna be here when ya do not
I ain't no monkey
Dis here ain' no show
I gave ya all I got
Nothin' here for ya; not no mo'
Ya walked out
Ya moved on
No need peepin'; tryin'na figga out wha goin' on
Fix ya neck and keep on movin'
Ya can't come back

Quit lookin' through ma winda
Ya won't like whatcha see
'Less ya can stomach someone else bein' close'ta me
Doin' whatcha used ta, but betta
Takin' care of all'la me
Bakin' cookies
Washin' dishes
Brick layin' at night

And recyclin' in da mornin'
Rinsin' and repeatin'
Doin' everything I like; exactly

Ya pic'chahs ain' on ma wall
Let's juss say they fall
Straight into da trash can
Ma phone won't take ya call
Ya been blocked, deleted, and all
Thank ya, mistah telephone man

Why ya lookin' through ma winda
Lookin' into ma life
Tryin'na see through ma soul
I hid nothin' from ya
Gave ya everthing I could
Seems the besta me wasn't good
Cause ma spirit, ya stole

No mem'ries and nothin' ta do wit ya any longa
Ma heart may be empty, but ma might is stronga

Ma winda's locked
And ma shades are pulled
Ain' nothin' for ya here
Ya said so
Ya made sho'
Ya left
Now, disappear

37

The Work

I've done most
And written the rest
I won't play a fool
For you or anyone else
I will be here alone
Before I put another before myself
That's a vow
A promise to you and me

I'm letting loose
I'm letting go
I'm letting you and all your shit flow
I don't need it
I don't want it
And I'm not taking it
This is my party
I say so

What didn't work
Wasn't meant to be

My heart is now open
Letting love and light flood into me
Experiencing a calmness and tranquility
That's been long overdue
Releasing you in every capacity
No feelings
No anger
No regrets
No resentment
No guilt
Making room for what's destined for me
Allowing myself to be completely free

I'm not discouraged
My spirit isn't broken
Feeling the strength
Loving the freedom
Empowered from the actions I've taken
Enlivened from the words I've spoken

From here on out
I'm living my life
And I'm writing the story
I state proudly
And I state firmly
I shall never be lonely
I've got love progressing all through me

38

Mirror, Mirror

When you look into the mirror
What do you see?
Is it what I see trying to holla at me?
Talk about a whole lot of scary

I'm not trying to be a brute
But from my point of view
You can't do a thing for me, boo
And that's not cute

Check yourself
Before you step to someone else
Get things straight
Make an honest effort
It doesn't have to be great
Just on the positive side of good
Give hope; show potential
The what if's...
The it could's...

Your new mantra
Repeat after me...

Fix My Life
Get It Right
Keep It Tight

Then repeat it twice, daily
Each morn at the break of day
And each night before being tucked away

Don't present yourself
Looking like a sore-eye sight
Think debonair, finesse, suave...
Leave Playa behind; roll Dynamite

Don't step to me with your game and seams unraveling
That's a highway I will not be traveling
To cruise in the left lane
You must hug the road
Set the pace
Know the speed
The limits you must exceed
Or pull to the right and move out of the way
I have places to be
And things to do
You're going nowhere
Anytime soon
I can't mess with you
I have needs
Make me fasten my seat belt
I want the best ride I can get

Standards
Preferences
Wants
Dislikes
Call them whatever
But too many mismatches
Are like basketball games and strikes
That just won't do

Put your best self forward
Don't do it for me
Do it for you
Play hardball
Get the reward
Show the world how you do

39

Iron In The Fire

That moment you regret opening your door
It's either for a cup of sugar or something more
Give. Give. Give.
Some people should forget where I live

You are no different
Why are you here?
Standing on my doorstep
Smiling from ear to ear

What do you want?
State your purpose
Let's be done with this

When you had me
You didn't want me
Now, I can't keep you away from me

I used to sit up at night
Sitting by the fire

Staring at the phone
Waiting for you to come home
Palms sweating
Knees twitching
Feet tapping on the floor
Completely filled with worry
Then you'd come in
Walking right past me
Like I wasn't there
Not a second thought
Not a single care

Now, you're just a nuisance
A pest
A leech – all up on me
The pain and suffering
I can hear it in your voice
You've realized it; you made the wrong choice

While I'd love to hear you babble
You miss me
You adore me
You can't live life without me
How much you love me
All kinds of bologna
You need to leave

I have company.

40

Auric

I'm not copper or silver
I am gold
I am the trophy
I exemplify the mold

There's a reason I am First
I'm multifaceted; I quench thirsts
I shine brighter than a sunbeam's burst

If I'm not the one you wake up to
Smiling in each other's face
Then the Runner-Up can take my place
Let the flashlight lead the way for you
That's the best thing for you to do

I'm not staying and settling for less
You can have your second best
I'm not about that mess

41

Pink Posty

It's over, baby
Your loss
One move and you threw it all away
Thinking you could come back another day
That's not the kind of game I play

I'm the boss
I don't need you here wasting space
Talking nonsense, breathing in my face
Step, step
Someone's taking your place

42

I Got Me

You have to be above me to upgrade me
You can't do that chasing after me, running beside me, lagging
behind me, and falling off
Find someone else to take care of
I got me

43

Glow

The limelight of love
Glows from within
I lost you, but it's a win-win

44

"Goodbye" [in French]

Your mouth speaks "yes"
But, it's the things you do...

I'll escort you to the door...
As I bid you adieu

45

POW!!!

Look at me now
Up until the day you die
You'll wonder how you could have me and let me go so easily

I wasn't special
You weren't drawn to me
I did nothing for you
I was common and ordinary
Bland as dry could be

Now, here we are
Pretend like you don't know if you want to
But, we both know it's true
You miss me, but I not you

46

❧

Pushing Up Daisies

My life's been upside down and it hasn't been the same
Since that warm night in November
When you sat down next to me
Held my hand in yours
Looked at me with a straight face
And said I wasn't what you needed

"We should be friends."

My heart stopped before it could beat, again
It was just the beginning
How could it be the end

My eyes flooded before I could reach the door
I needed some air
I'd never wanted anything more

You look into my eyes
You know that I still love you
I look into yours

Someone else is sparkling there

I held on too long
Hoping you'd come back to me
Three years later, I learned how you actually felt
The worse hand I have ever been dealt
You said there was no chemistry
No connection
No reason to be with me
But, it wasn't me
We would be better as friends
I think, you meant friend-ly

Your behavior tells me so
I think it's time I let you know:

Your words say, "I'll be there"
Your actions say, "I don't care"

From here, we go where?
I've done all I know to do
The next step is on you

If you ever need me, I'll be around
But, the time has come for me to lay this down
Put us to rest
Wherever life may lead us
I wish you the best

47

180

The wind was blowing
The rain was falling
The streetlights had the city glistening
You were beside me; my insides were glowing
I was cozy; holding on to you
Absorbing your words; listening
As my mind drifted into space
My eyes began to swell
My heart crumbled
My face fell
You said we needed a change of pace

There was no slowing down
You just stopped
And walked off in the opposite direction

Not once have you looked back
Not once have you come back
Not once have you called back
To you...that was that

Proof you can forget what you once knew
And some things simply mean nothing to you

48

Shoo

No more holding on
This is where I let you go
I rebuke you
I release you
I refuse to be connected to you
Shoo fly, shoo

I don't need you sticking around
Hovering in my space
Landing on my walls
Flying around my pots
Serving no purpose; adding no value
Just getting in the way
Contaminating my life

Gone are the days where I lose me to put you first
Never again will I feed you before quenching my own thirst
I'm not who I used to be
This is the real me
I stand tall

I stand proud
I stand strong
What's right is you're wrong
And I thank you
Now, get gone
Fly away

I'm done giving you my all
And getting nothing in return
My love and my life aren't free
They must be earned

Move on
Be gone
You do you
I got me
Now, shoo!

49

Oil + Vinegar

Don't think you know me
Because you don't

I have things you want
Again, you don't

What I wanted, I got
What I have, I earned
You haven't
You won't

Stop with the jealousy
It's a waste of time and energy
We are no comparison
Find something better to do
I don't want to be you
And you could never be me

My life may appear to be peaches & cream, comfort & luxury,
blue orchids & red roses

It's not
The glitter & gold come in manageable doses
My blood flows and my heart aches
I know my strengths and I know what all I can take
I may stumble
But I will not break
I am human
I like hugs
I make mistakes

My life is filled with blue and sunny skies
But I have days of stormy weather
I keep my life together
I keep it simple
I don't do drama and I'm an adult
I act like so
I leave the games to the kids
I teach them and lead by example
A diagram; a way for them to know

What happens in my house
Stays within my home
I'm not a news network
I don't broadcast my business and I keep my lips zipped
What happens in Harlem doesn't need to air in Rome
If you're a part of the story
You'll know the script

Stop the envy
Save the hate
It'll never faze me
Go control your own destiny
Seal your own fate

Stop wanting to be me
Be your best version of great

50

Antiquity

I'm so over you
I don't know who you are
Like footprints in the sand
Memories of you have been washed away
You were then, back in the day
When I sketched us in my notebook
Played MASH and X's & O's
Guessed how many years we would be
Drew graffiti on my jackets and jeans
Scribbled hearts all around your name
And wrote love letters asking you to check "yes" or "no"
A young lover's mind
I wish that was all it took

But, no more; I've left all that there
I'm not going back
I'm not changing my direction or going out of my way
Just to see your face and hope you have something to say
You will never ruin another day

I would blush when I saw you
And lose all ability to speak
Like an out-of-body experience
I couldn't tell who was who
Didn't even know if I was me

Yet, I knew you
You kept it true
Not once have you changed your tune
Kept on doing you
That was the child in me
Adoring your scheme
Not seeing past what I wanted to be
I'm grown now
I'm done toying with you
Enjoy your adolescent games
I've moved on

So long.

51

I.HATE.YOU.

It's plain.
It's simple.
It's that easily stated.

I put my life on hold for you
Like a fool
I waited

For you to realize I was the one
For you to accomplish goals in life and have time for me
For you to reach out and wrap your arms around me
For you to look at me and a smile grow on your face
For you to be better and to do better
You did neither

I waited
For life to pass me by
It did at record pace

For the time to come for me to open my eyes

It did when I could breathe and not cry

For the moment when I could think of you and not hurt anymore
It did
The instant I let you go and knew that I would be okay

I am fine
I am me

I don't love you
Don't even like you like I used to
I hate you

The thought of you.
The sight of you.
The smell of you.
The memory of you.
The essence of you.
The marrow in you.
The all of you.
The you of you.

YOU.

52

You Don't Even Know

When I give you my all
Tell you the truth
And show you who I am
I am still not enough

If I invested in me
The time I spend on you
There's so much that I could do
So much more that I could be

I don't need you
Weighing me down
Holding me back
Blocking me from being me
I'm doing what you think I should
Becoming what you want me to be
Seeing life from your point of view
That's a bogus version of you
Not the best representation of me

Leave me as I am
I can thrive on my own
You aren't the melody or the lyrics to my song

The music's in me
Giving me strength
Giving me courage
Moving me to where I belong
Overcoming my fear
Humming as I move along
Turning right from a wrong

53

Get

Did you expect my life to stop
My face to crack
My world to crumble
When you said I should find someone else to love
Someone for me
One to love me the way I deserve to be

I didn't want you to speak for me
Passing your opinions as mine
Spewing lines that never came to mind
Words that would never cross my tongue
Saying what I would and wouldn't do
I form words
I make statements
I validate points
I have a voice
I leave no song unsung
I'm not asking you to save me
You're not a savior
I don't need you to protect me

You're not Frank Farmer
I'm taken care of
My life's wrapped in spiritual armor
You wanted to support me
I've come this far without you
I'm doing okay

Your purpose was to be my friend
Like a lover should be
To be my partner
Where I could share my life with you
And you share yours with me
Our hearts; two, beating as one
All you had to do was play your part
To just be you
But that was too great
Something else you couldn't do

But, I digress
Allow me to confess
I have someone
I've always had that someone
I am the one
I love me
I love me more than you ever could
I love me enough for you, too
So, I send self-love, fulfillment, and freedom to you
Certified-Mail; keep the receipt

54

Closure Letter

Dear Unforgettable:

I know it's been a while since we've seen each other
But I see you often
In my nightmares, in my daydreams
In the faces of strangers as I'm walking down the street
In fields of trees bending into a breeze
In reflecting upon moments of my past
I saw you the other day
But couldn't bring myself to approach you
Like usual, you took my breath away
You look great
Sexier than ever
Your smile still makes me sway

Living without you hasn't been easy
But I did what I thought was best
For you and for me

I've never been attracted to someone

The way I was to you
You broadened my horizons
Introduced me to plenty and new
Showed me how to live
Looking at life from a unique point of view
Through the eyes of You

Your not hearing from me
Doesn't mean I don't think of you
Doesn't mean I don't care
I love you
I love you enough to let you go
To let you live your life
To be that great person that you don't need me in order to be

Leaving you was hard to do
Staying away is even harder
But, I carry you with me
You'll always have a special place
In my memories and in my heart
Live your life
Remember what you taught me

You...I will never forget

Warmly,

The One You Gave Your Heart To

55

Objects

You chose new
While I chose you
The memories
The laughter
The tears
The fears
All gone
Meant nothing to you
Not even a glimpse to be caught in your rearview
Should you choose to look behind you

56

Love Into Being

Life and love are gifts
Enjoy the present
Live in the now
There may be no next hour

Speak to my soul
Not my body
Deliver the sensational
The uncautionary
The unconditional love story

Believe in it
Get lost in it

Let's breathe without losing our breath
Hold on to air; forbidding its escape
Let's fight the point that's make or break

Make it
Define it

What we have...is it

Let it be love

57

Fed Up

The arguing stops when there's nothing left to be said
Why keep you around when there's nothing for you to do
You serve no purpose
You have no use
That's like being weak, yet, refusing to let things loose

I'm not going to fight with you
When you have nothing I want
I'm not going to fight for you
When you aren't who I want

I no longer desire your apology
You can keep it
Along with your excuses and sob stories
What you did may not have been done maliciously
But you did it...
Intentionally
Selfishly
No regard for me
No respect for us

As always, everything was about you

I won't be smiling in your face
I won't be talking about you to anyone
No thoughts of you shall ever come
The war is over
The damage is done
Trust and believe
Rest and be assured
I'll never think of you anymore

58

One of Those Moments

Why are you looking at me
Expecting me to care
You said it yourself
With you, there's nothing for me there
My performance is done
My bags are packed
I am long gone
You'll have to live life on your own
I can't help you

59

Victory

Staring into the mirror; waving a white flag
The pain, the hurt...they don't fade away
I've been there; I've done that
I know all the rest
I'm not doing it and I'm not taking it, either
This has to end or I will never win
Don't get up
I can see myself to the door

60

Two Cents' Worth

For the truth shall unfold and be revealed
Be careful of the lies you freely spiel
You do it so easily, so naturally
You convince yourself
Be great today
You don't know what tomorrow may hold

61

Forever Came

For the truth shall unfold and be revealed
Be careful

I never would've thought you could instantly be gone
away from me
I am grateful for the time we spent
For the wrath between us created a better me
You've shown me bad and given me worse
Someone else can show me well and give me better
I'll treat me best

When love wasn't enough
I realized I didn't see it because I didn't want to believe it
It wasn't what it used to be
There wasn't anything to get back
There wasn't anything to go back to

I had passed the point of wanting to scream until your soul
spoke words of declaration
I no longer wanted to dance until your heart beat to thoughts

of me
I was done
Our time had come and gone
I'm not sure if it came too fast or took too long
But, Forever came
And I don't care if you remember or forget about me

62

#Swerve

Don't dial my number when you don't know my name
I'm not your enemy
And I'm not your friend
So call someone else to play your insecurity game

Don't worry about whose chain I'm wearing
Whose car I'm driving
Or whose jacket I'm wrapped in
How are you getting home?
How are you keeping warm?
I have mine; do you have your own?

Stop wondering about what my Love and I do
Handle things between you and your boo
I don't want your raggedy ass man
If I did, he wouldn't know you

I don't do sideline cheers or walk-on parts
That's where the drama starts
I'm the center of attention

The one the playbill and the marquis mention
I own the name everyone knows
I'm the one who's presented with a rose

You're so consumed with jealousy
You don't know if you hate me
Or if you want to be me
It's okay to dream
But embrace reality: You're confused
Getting my life and your hallucination twisted
Going out of your way to find numbers unlisted
Before you reach out to dial my phone
Ask yourself why your man ain' home
Then ask him.

63

raison d'être

I don't have to look any further
After you there could never stand another

I smile when I'm in your presence
Taking you in
Anticipating what you'll do
My heart thumping
My pulse pumping
My hands shaking
My breath, I'm holding
Passing points where I'm normally breaking
Only you can faze me
Only you make me feel like this

I mean the most to you
I'm the one
The one that's worth more than gold
You've told me so
In the things you say
All I've been told

All that you do
All that's been done
The way you touch me in the small of my back and pull me close
The way you handle me in that special way
Making me lose all bodily control
The magic in your words serenades my soul
Soaps my body
Washes between my toes
Takes me to that place of release
My private getaway
My personal acquiesce

You stimulate and validate me
Catering to my needs
You set fire to my pain
You blow away the ashes of my past
The way you caress my face
Kiss my lips
Enjoy my hips
The way you sway with me
Groove with me
Dance with me
The way we fuel our fire and feel our burn
The way we give
The way we get
The way we love in return

Chivalry is alive, surrounding me in comfort and ease
Opening doors, doing what my daddy said a good one would
Stopping by to hug me tight
Making sure I have a pleasant night
Phoning in the morning to hear me breathe
Many pray for a lover like you

The motive for a caged bird's song
You are my blessing
Yet, so much more

Your essence is a seductive tease
A melody
A love song
A soundtrack
A complement to all of me

64

ROI (Return On Investment)

You can leave
Someone else can have you
All I've done for you
Everything I've given you
I call it an investment
A testament to the genius I am

Do as you will
I got money on the table
You'll always be mine
You're weak and you're strengthless
You have the legs
But to be You, you have to be free and stable
You ain' able

You reached where you are
Because of who I am

I took you in
Gave you everything when you had nothing

I was your strength, your spirit, and your income
I never asked for anything in return
Despite your lack of interest and not one generated dividend

In the end, I'll get what's rightfully due me
You benefited, but I'm the beneficiary

65

No Longer

No longer are you the danger to my soul
Or the thought that makes me weak
I found strength in losing you and got stronger by getting over you

No longer am I afraid to confront or express my shortcomings
I now embrace all that makes me who I am
The complete picture
The icing on the cake
The sundae and the cherry on top
I made the cake, I sliced the cake, I served the cake
I'm gonna eat the cake too

No longer am I following your lead or waiting for you to tell me
where I belong
This is my life; I'll make my own place and sing my own
celebration song

66

Miss Me, I'm Gone

I'm leaving; I'm never coming back
Grabbing my keys
Slamming the door
Pushing metal to the floor

Remember my scent like a love song
That seductive tease
The therapy that puts all your troubles at ease

You don't miss me, now
But, in time you will
You're gonna wonder
How do you let me go
When I'm already gone and you're the only one holding one

You're gonna miss me
But, baby...I'm gone

67

It's Over

It's over
I set peace to my life
Freed the pain
Had to let you be
Had to do me

68

Over My Shoulder

You were everything to me back in the day
Been gone so long I forgot about you
A distant memory
Come back to haunt me
Pressing into me
Whispering how much you want me
I question the value of your words like all the things you say

You continue to wonder how you lived without me
You asked yourself this every single day
How did we get here, how did things become this way

Objects in the mirror, are they closer than they appear
That's my thought, whether it's sunny or gray

The new me
The one who replaced me
The one across the view
Pretending not to see you
Trying to ignore you

Looking awkward, unable to figure out what to do
This is me, but never who I wanted to be

69

You In Us

Your touch melts my core
Your smile drops me from the clouds to the floor
Your looks say I am sex appeal
Your kisses say you can't get enough of me
I keep you filled and you give me more
I am your moth
You are my flame

Your hand heals when it travels across my body
Your fingers slide
Your tongue glides
Your love envelops me in safety and warmth
Your words speak a truth that's unheard
Your actions paint a picture
A vision of beauty to behold

In you I have everything
And in everything there's you
The whipped cream, the cherry
You're my sugar on top

When never too much is a good thing and too much
is never enough

Me in you
And you in Me

We in Us.

70

Me Because of You

I'd been lost so long
I'd become comfortable and called it Home
You dug me out of the unknown
Straight into your arms
Warm and strong
It's like being held and holding on

You clutch my hand and my heart lights up
You look into my eyes and I see tomorrow
You whisper into my ears and I hear what I imagine Heaven to be
You kiss me
I taste you
My spine tingles
My body explodes
You unleash my secrets
Spilling truths no one knows
Unveiling news that's new to me

You don't bring me worry
You don't gift me pain

You wipe away my tears
You drive away my fears
You kiss away the affliction and strain
Give me reasons to let love remain
To let it live and let it breathe
To let it sing
To let it soar
To let it be an encore

My life's moving to a new beat
The music in you has set me free
Turning me into someone I never thought I could be
A new and better me

71

You

You changed my life
You opened my eyes
You lit my fire
You built my desire

I've come to crave your touch
The way you drape your arm across me and pull me close
Holding me, all through the night
Sleep so peaceful
Like what I imagine Heaven to be

I feel safe when I'm with you
Like nothing else matters when I'm in your view
Your lips placed, gently, upon mine
Our eyes dancing until they shine

My heart jumps
Your happiness flows through me
It's like I've known you for a lifetime
But there's still so much time

Time for us to grow
Everything about you
All of it, I want to know

I'm so blessed to have you in my life
Everything...all of a sudden
It all feels so right
The loves from the past
So wrong then
Seem right at last
Things are taken away
To make room for what's best for you
Brightening an already perfect day

72

"I Love You, Back!"

Remembering the Diamond Standard...

Whitney Elizabeth Houston
(Aug. 9, 1963 – Feb. 11, 2012)

My songbird has spread her wings
And taken that heavenly flight
Leaving behind a legacy bathed in stardust, triumph, history,
and spotlight

I look to you up above
Smiling brightly
Singing sweetly
I see your halo sparkling
Its light reaching all the way here
Helping me cherish memories that keep you near
My eyes watering each time I hear you sing

From the moment I first heard you
I completely lost my mind
You were a miracle and transcendent standard
Realities deemed unattainable and unfathomable

You were The Voice
Indescribable.
Incomparable.
The Eighth Wonder of the world.
Everyone knew you were My Girl

Your talent was music to my ears
It fed my soul
Energized my spirit
It was the soft, loving touch
That wiped away my tears
It hugged me. It held me.
It wrapped me in comfort and ease
All that I could want
All that I could need
Your skill heals me when my soul needs repair
Your voice surrounds me in moments of despair
Those moments in time
When I know you'll always be there

When I have nothing, you're all over me
Giving good love
Keeping me strong
Giving me the strength to carry on

Many will always love you
But nobody loves you like I do

I salute you.

Rest In Peace, Nippy.
You are loved and will forever be missed.

Acknowledgements & Thank You's

Mama (Elnora S. Locklair); thank you, thank you, thank you...for life...for love...for everything. I love and miss you more than words can say. RIP.

Daddy; you know, you're alright. Keep your nose clean! Love me some you.

My Big Sister Gorgeous One, Tanya (Mwah); and my big bro, La'Mont (cockadoodle-dooo!).

Jen-Jen; thanks for the ever-lasting love and support. I love you more! Donkey, I love and miss you so much....RIP.

My Cri-Tique-Crew:
Quiana Parler (you know how we do), Deidre Brown (you live my life, so I'm telling all of your business), Kim Smith (loving you always, Delicious! RIP), Sonja Smith (we're twins in every lifetime), Jezula Antoine (Plant me now!), Lacy Anderson (rivers and disco balls!), Kim Johnson (we're still doing it), Derrick Deberry (give me that Whitney note and Beyonce snap), and Patricia Wilcox (the lives we have lived!). SMOOCHES!

My peeps who cheered me on in various ways throughout this long journey:
Tina Bernard, Patty Greene-Maher, Aimée Bivins, Jared 'J-Ry' Smith, Tariq M. Walker, Bridget Parkinson, Lolita Files (me, Penn Hamilton, and our own story...work that out! #xoxo), Nicole Childers, Juan

Gaddis, Jen Pearson, Lolita Miller, Jon Gazarek, Steve Gallion (I'm coming for your swag...wherever you are!), Nick Heyward, Priscilla Adjei, and Lisa Alexander.

Ty, Keya, Shyla, and Aaliyah: You give me more love than you'll ever know.

And a special thanks to YOU. Thank you for loving me, supporting me, and for taking the time to read this collection (and the other two?). I love your taste! Enjoy!

As you may already know, much of my work is "inspired in part by" some significant motivational force in my life (i.e., family, friends, love [and the pursuit of], relationships [or things similar in nature], opinions and outlooks on EVERYTHING, and the many aspects of life that shape us all into our individual, wonderful selves).

Feel free to write me, tweet me, or slide into the DMs; or get whatever info you need to send me money and gifts. I still do email: SayingsOfASoul@yahoo.com. If I don't write you, I'll write you! ☺

Nothin' but love.... **@syievelocklair**

Sealed with a kiss...

Before you turn this last page, allow me to say thank you, thank you, thank yooouuuuuu! I appreciate you taking this journey with me: three collections, hundreds of pages, some tears, and far too many years.

I admit: I held on to *Singing My Own Song* for a long time before letting it breathe; it never felt complete. Was I still dealing with something? Were emotions left unchecked? Were poems incomplete? Was there more to say? All questions I had, but their answers never seemed to be THE answer. [Guardian Angel re-enters with a Hallelujah Moment Conversation.] It hit me! I somehow excluded some very special acknowledgments across the collections. No idea how I did that.

There are two wonderfully-magnificent people who were forces that encouraged me to be myself, to express myself, and motivated me to continue writing and sharing my work – at least with friends; never knew if they meant publicly, but ... you know ... dream big! I'm hoping they saw some reason in the rhyme and some rhythm mixed within.

Mrs. Meochia Ford and Mr. Thomas Bonnet; my heart and soul overflow because of you. Thank you for your support and encouraging me to be my best, to do my best, to not be afraid of myself, to be different and stand out from the crowd, and to use and share my gifts. Because of you, I can 'sing' (and sway) to my own song. I'm not touching the music part, though. ;-)